MY BEAUTITIFUL WIFE

The Love of my Life

KELVIN DOVE

Table of contents

Chapter 1

Introduction

I am grateful to be able to call the most wonderful and beautiful woman in the world my wife. She is the love of my life, and I am so blessed to have her by my side. From the moment we met, I knew that she was someone special, and I am grateful to have her as my partner in life. My wife is kind, compassionate, and understanding, and she brings so much joy and happiness into my life. She is the reason for my smile, and I am grateful for everything she does for me and our family. I am lucky to have such an amazing wife, and I am grateful to be able to call her mine.

I could not be more in love with my beautiful wife. She is not only stunning on the outside, but her inner beauty radiates even more brightly. From the moment I met her, I knew that she was someone special, and I have been in awe of her ever since.

My wife has a heart of gold, and she is always there to support and encourage me. She is my best friend, my confidant, and my partner in every sense of the word. She makes my life complete, and I am so grateful to have her by my side.

Whether we're spending time with our family and friends, working on a project together, or just enjoying a quiet night at home, I know that I can always count on her to be there for me. Her loving and caring nature is a true inspiration to me, and I know that I am a better person for having her in my life.

I am so lucky to have such an amazing wife, and I am grateful to be able to call her mine. I love her with all my heart and I know that she is truly the love of my life.

Chapter 2

The Beginning of Our Love Story

It was a typical day at the office when I first laid eyes on her. She walked in, and everything else seemed to fade away. I couldn't take my eyes off of her. She was beautiful, and there was just something about her that drew me in.

As fate would have it, we were introduced by a mutual friend and I knew from that moment on that I wanted to get to know her better. We talked and laughed all afternoon, and I felt an instant connection with her.

As we got to know each other, I learned more about her, and I fell more and more in love with her. She was smart, funny, and kind-hearted, and she had a passion for life that was infectious. I couldn't believe that I had found such an amazing woman, and I knew that I wanted to spend the rest of my life with her.

I finally worked up the courage to ask her out on a date, and she said yes. That was the beginning of our love story. It wasn't always easy, but we knew we were meant to be together. Our love grew stronger with each passing day, and soon we were inseparable.

I knew that I wanted to spend the rest of my life with her, and I proposed to her on a beach at sunset. She said yes, and we were married in a beautiful ceremony surrounded by our loved ones.

It's been an amazing journey since that day, and I wouldn't change a thing. My beautiful wife is my best friend, my confidant, and my partner in every sense of the word. I am so grateful to have her by my side, and I know that our love will continue to grow stronger with each passing day.

Our first date was unforgettable, it was a simple dinner at a local restaurant, but the conversation was effortless and we talked for hours. From that day on we started dating and spent every moment together, getting to know each other more and more. I was smitten by her intelligence, her sense of humor and her kind heart. We had an instant connection, a special bond that was undeniable.

As we moved forward in our relationship, we faced our fair share of obstacles, but we always found a way to work through them. We supported each other through tough times, and we celebrated our joys together. I knew that she was the one for me and I couldn't imagine my life without her.

When we were dating, we talked about our future, our goals and aspirations, and it was clear that we were on the same path. We had a shared vision for our lives together, and I knew that we were meant to be.

The day I proposed to her was one of the best days of my life. It was a beautiful summer afternoon, and we were sitting by the lake. I got down on one knee and asked her to be my wife. She was surprised and overjoyed, and she said yes. It was a moment that I will treasure forever.

We got married in a beautiful ceremony surrounded by our loved ones. It was a day that I will always remember, the day that I married the love of my life.

Since then, we've been together for a number of years and our love has only grown stronger. My wife continues to be my best friend, my confidant, and my partner in every sense of the word. I am grateful for her, and I know that our love will continue to be a source of joy, strength and inspiration in my life.

Chapter 3

Building Our Life Together

After we got married, we set out to build a life together. We bought a house, got a dog and started working on our careers. It wasn't always easy, but we did it together. My wife is a hard worker and she always had a vision for what she wanted. She was able to pursue her dreams, and I was always there to support her.

With her encouragement, I was able to make a career change and find a job that I love. We were building a future together and everything was falling into place.

We also started a family and had children. My wife was an amazing mother and she was able to balance her career and her role as a mother, she was truly an inspiration. Our children were the center of our world and brought so much joy and love to our lives.

As our family grew, we faced new challenges, but we were determined to make it work. My wife was always there to lend a hand, to listen, and to offer her support. I knew that I could count on her, and I knew that she could count on me.

We were building our life together and it was a beautiful thing. We shared a deep love, and we knew that we would face anything together as a team.

We enjoyed our time as a family, traveling, laughing and making memories together, we faced the good times and the bad times as a team, and we always came out stronger. Our love for each other was the foundation of our lives, and it gave us the strength to face anything that came our way.

I was grateful to have such an amazing wife by my side, and I knew that our love would continue to be a source of joy and strength in my life. As we settled into our new life together, we made sure to make time for each other, even amidst the busyness of daily life. We went on trips and made special memories, from romantic getaways to family vacations, we always found time to create special moments.

We also made sure to make time for date nights, even when we were busy with work and kids, it was important for us to keep the spark alive.

We also supported each other in our individual pursuits and interests. My wife is a creative soul and she had a passion for painting, she started taking classes and eventually had her first exhibition, I was so proud of her and I was happy to see her pursue her passions. I was inspired by her, and I knew that our relationship was one of mutual support and encouragement.

As we built our life together, we faced hardships and difficult times, but we always leaned on each other. We knew that we could count on each other no matter what. Our love for each other gave us the strength to face any challenge that came our way.

Our love and partnership continues to be the backbone of our family and our life together. We're grateful to have each other and our love has only grown stronger with time. I know that my wife is my forever and I am so thankful to have her by my side.

Chapter 4

Our Life Together

After we got married, our life together was filled with love, laughter and a whole lot of adventure. We traveled to different parts of the world, and made memories that will last a lifetime. We explored new cultures and met new people, and each trip we took brought us even closer together.

As we settled into our new life together, we were blessed with two beautiful children. My wife was an amazing mother, always putting her children first and creating a loving and nurturing environment for them to grow up in. She was a devoted wife and partner, and together we were raising a beautiful family.

Being a parent was a whole new experience for both of us, and we learned so much about ourselves and each other. We would often have late-night talks, discussing our parenting styles and figuring out how to raise our children in the best way possible. My wife always brought calm and understanding to our discussions and was the voice of reason when things got tough.

In the midst of raising a family and building a life together, we also worked hard to maintain our relationship. We made sure to take time for each other, to keep the spark alive and to always communicate openly and honestly. We have always been each other's best friend, and that bond has only grown stronger over time.

Now, as we look back on our life together, we realize that we have built a beautiful life. We have shared so many experiences, laughed so many laughs and cried so many tears together. We are truly blessed to have each other, and I know that our love will continue to grow stronger with each passing day.

We have built a beautiful life together and I can't wait to see what the future holds for us. I am grateful for my beautiful wife and the love we share; I know that she will always be the love of my life.

As we built our life together, my wife and I faced many challenges and overcome them. We have faced financial hardships, health issues, and family emergencies, but through it all, we have always had each other to lean on. My wife has been my rock, my support and my confidant through everything, and I knew that I could always count on her.

We also faced some moments of doubt and insecurity in our relationship, but we were always honest and open with each other. We communicated effectively and worked through our issues together. Our love for each other was always stronger than any problems that we faced, and we knew that we were meant to be together.

In addition to our family, we also had a strong network of friends and family who supported us through our journey. We are grateful for their love and support, and we knew that we couldn't have done it without them.

As we look back on our life together, we realize that we have built a beautiful life. We have shared so many experiences, laughed so many laughs and cried so many tears together. We have built a beautiful home, a loving family, and a strong relationship. Our love has been tested, but it has only grown stronger over time.

My wife is not just my partner in life, but also my best friend, my confidant and my soul mate. I am grateful for her, and I know that our love will continue to be a source of joy, strength, and inspiration in my life. I am truly blessed to have her as my wife, and I am looking forward to many more years of love and happiness together.

As our family grew, we faced many new challenges, but also many new joys and celebrations. Watching our children grow up and become their own individuals was a truly rewarding experience. We laughed together, cried together, and shared so many precious moments that we will never forget. My wife was an amazing mother, always putting her children first and creating a loving and nurturing environment for them to grow up in.

In addition to raising our children, my wife and I also made sure to make time for each other. We made date nights a priority and would often plan trips or special outings just for the two of us. It's important to have time alone, away from the stresses of everyday life, to reconnect and remember why we fell in love in the first place.

As our children grew older and became more independent, we started to have more time for each other and to focus on our relationship. It was a different kind of bond now, one that had grown and evolved over the years. We had a deeper understanding of each other and an unbreakable trust. My wife was not just my partner in life, but also my best friend, my confidant and my soul mate.

We have had an amazing journey together, and I am grateful for every moment of it. As we look ahead to the future, I know that our love will continue to grow and flourish. My wife will always be the love of my life and I am grateful to have her by my side for every step of the way.

Chapter 4

A Future Together

As I think about the future with my wife, I know that our love will only continue to grow stronger. I can't wait to see what the future holds for us and for our family.

We have always been a team and we have supported each other through everything. We have seen each other through the good times and the bad, and I know that we will continue to do so in the future.

One of the things I am most excited about is growing old together. Seeing my wife aged gracefully and experiencing the little joys and challenges of aging together. We have built a life together that I am proud of, and I can't wait to continue to build more memories together in the coming years.

We also have plans to travel more in the future; we have talked about visiting different countries and experiencing new cultures. It's exciting to think about all the adventures we will have together, and all the memories we will make.

In addition to traveling, we are also looking forward to watching our children grow and start families of their own. We can't wait to be grandparents and to watch our family grow.

My wife has always been my rock, my support, and my confidant. She makes my life complete, and I am so grateful to have her by my side. I am looking forward to spending the rest of my life with her, and I know that our love will continue to be a source of joy, strength, and inspiration in my life.

I am truly blessed to have her as my wife, and I am excited for all the adventures, joys, and challenges that the future holds for us. I know that with my beautiful wife by my side, anything is possible.

As my wife and I look forward to the future, we are filled with optimism and excitement. We have been through so much together and have grown stronger as a result. We have a deep understanding and trust in each other and know that no matter what the future holds, we will always be there for each other.

One of the things we are most excited about is the prospect of being empty nesters. We have loved being parents and watching our children grow into wonderful adults, but now it's time for us to focus on each other again and rediscover the love that brought us together in the first place. We are looking forward to the freedom and flexibility that comes with having grown-up children, and being able to travel and explore new places together.

We also look forward to being more active in our community and giving back in ways that we haven't been able to before. We want to make a positive impact and leave a lasting legacy in the world.

As we think about our future together, I am reminded of how grateful I am to have my beautiful wife by my side. She has been my rock, my support and my confidant throughout our life together. I know that our love will continue to be a source of

As we look to the future, my wife and I are filled with excitement and anticipation. We have built a strong foundation together, and know that no matter what the future holds, we will face it together. We have grown to understand each other and trust each other, and our love has only grown stronger as a result.

Also we are most excited about is the prospect of having more time to travel and explore new places together. We have always enjoyed traveling and have shared many wonderful experiences together. We have many places we still want to visit and adventures we still want to have.

In addition to travelling, we are also looking forward to the next stage of our lives and giving back to our community. We want to use our time and resources to make a positive impact and help others in need. We want to make a difference in the world and leave a lasting legacy.

As we think about our future together, I am reminded of how grateful I am to have my wife by my side. She has been my rock, my support, and my confidant throughout our life together. I know that our love will continue to be a source of strength and inspiration in our lives. She is truly my everything, and I cannot wait to see what the future holds for us.

Conclusion

As I reflect on my life and my love for my wife, I am filled with gratitude and appreciation. She is the love of my life, my best friend and my soul mate. From the moment I met her, I knew that she was special, and as I got to know her, I fell deeply in love with her.

Over the years, we have built a beautiful life together. We have faced challenges and overcome them, we have laughed and cried together, and we have shared so many precious moments that I will always treasure. My wife has been my rock, my support and my confidant throughout our journey together.

As we look ahead to the future, I know that our love will continue to grow and flourish. We have plans for more travel, and more opportunities to make new memories together. We are excited to see our children grow and start families of their own and to be a part of their lives. We also look forward to giving back to our community and making a positive impact in the world.

I am truly blessed to have my beautiful wife as my partner in life. She is my everything and I am grateful to have her by my side. I am looking forward to spending many more years of love and happiness with her and I know that our love will continue to be a source of joy, strength and inspiration in my life. I thank you for reading my love story; I am forever thankful and blessed to have her in my life.

My wife is not just my partner in life, but also my best friend, my confidant, and my soul mate. She is the love of my life, and I am grateful for every moment we have shared together.

Throughout our journey together, we have faced challenges, but we have always come out stronger. We have laughed and cried together, and we have shared so many precious moments that I will always treasure. My wife has been my rock, my support, and my confidant throughout our journey together.

As we look ahead to the future, I know that our love will continue to grow and flourish. We have plans to travel more and to make more memories together. We are excited to watch our children grow and start families of their own and to be a part of their lives. We also look forward to giving back to our community and making a positive impact in the world.

I am truly blessed to have my beautiful wife by my side. She is my everything, and I am grateful to have her in my life. I am looking forward to spending many more years of love and happiness with her and to building a beautiful life together. I am thankful for the love we share, and for the story of our love that will live on forever.

www.ingramcontent.com/pod-product-compliance
Lightning Source LLC
LaVergne TN
LVHW020545160826
845677LV00015B/4210

9798373353540